How Does Earth's Surface Change?

Houghton Mifflin Harcourt™

PHOTOGRAPHY CREDITS: COVER (bg) ©Stan Rohrer/Alamy Images; 3 (b) ©Dennis Albert Richardson/Shutterstock; 4 (t) ©Stan Rohrer/Alamy Images; 5 (b) ©David Wall Photography/Lonely Planet Images/Getty Images; 6 (b) Photodisc/Getty Images; 7 (r) ©Corbis; 8 (t) ©Getty Images; 9 (bg) Dusty Pixel Photography/FlickrGetty Images; 10 (b) ©Bjorn Holland/The Image Bank/Getty Images; 12 (b) ©Kenneth Garrett/National Geographic/Getty Images; 13 (t) ©ribeiroantonio/Shutterstock; 14 (t) ©Jo Ingate/Alamy Images; 15 (t) ©Siede Preis/Photodisc/Getty Images; 16 (l) ©Marcio Jose Bastos Silva/Shutterstock; 16 (r) ©Purestock/Getty Images; 17 (r) ©John Warburton-Lee/AWL Images/Getty Images; 19 (b) ©Chris Saulit/Flickr/Getty Images; 21 (r) © H. David Seawell/Corbis

Printed in the U.S.A.

ISBN: 978-0-544-07340-1

16 17 18 19 20 1083 20 19 18

4500710588 B C D E F

Be an Active Reader!

Look for each word in yellow along with its meaning.

weathering	fossil	index fossil
erosion	mold	mass extinction
sedimentary rock	cast	fossil fuel
deposition		

Underlined sentences answer the questions.

What are landforms?
What are weathering and erosion?
How can weathering and erosion form canyons?
How does deposition cause deltas and sand dunes?
How is sedimentary rock formed?
How are fossils formed?
What can fossils tell us about organisms of the past?
How do organisms of the past compare to organisms today?
How can fossils tell us about Earth's history?
What happens when organisms do not become fossils?

What are landforms?

Earth's surface is always changing. Many different kinds of places are parts of Earth's surface. The tops of mountains and the bottoms of oceans are part of Earth's surface. So are beaches and deserts. Even the tiny stones that break off big rocks are part of Earth's surface.

Landforms are the natural features formed by changes on Earth's surface. Mountains, valleys, hills, cliffs, and plains are all landforms. Landforms are made and shaped by many different processes that happen over millions of years.

Moving water, wind, and ice are forces that have shaped Earth's landforms. These forces can build up the land. They can also tear down the land.

This rock arch was formed by wind and water. These forces wore away at the rock over thousands of years.

This rock has been changed by a glacier. The glacier's movement weathered the rock.

What are weathering and erosion?

Weathering is the breaking down of rock into smaller pieces. Water, wind, and ice are the main causes of weathering.

During winter, water gets into cracks in rock. Then the water freezes. The ice expands and breaks open the rock. Water causes weathering in other ways, too. Water in a river keeps washing over rock. After a long time, the rock wears away.

Wind can wear down rough rock and make it smooth. Ice can also wear away rock. A glacier wears rock away and breaks it apart as it moves. Chemicals can also cause rocks to crumble. Even living things such as tree roots can grow into rocks and break them apart. The process of weathering is natural. It is what makes Earth's landforms change over time.

Erosion is the process of moving weathered rock from one place to another. Weathering and erosion work together. For example, when snow melts on a mountain in spring, the water rushes down the mountain. This water carries sediment along. Sediment is sand, silt, small pieces of rock, and other bits of weathered matter. The sediment is deposited in new locations. This process is called deposition, the dropping or settling of eroded material.

Beaches experience a lot of erosion over time. Waves hit the shoreline over and over. The waves break up rock into sediment that the water washes away. The water carries the material to another place. Parts of the shoreline can disappear because of this erosion.

Erosion carries beach materials to new locations.

How can weathering and erosion form canyons?

Some landforms are caused by weathering and erosion. A canyon is a deep cut between cliffs of rock. A canyon is formed by a river over a long period of time. First, the river forms sediment when it weathers rock in the riverbed. The sediment weathers the sides and bottom of the riverbed during erosion. Over time, the riverbed becomes a deep groove. The groove gets so deep that a canyon forms.

A river's constant movement can cause the riverbed to weather and erode.

Canyons may be large or small. They take a long time to form. The Grand Canyon in Arizona is one of the largest canyons. It was formed by the Colorado River. If you look down into the canyon from high above, the Colorado River looks tiny. It looks that way because the canyon is almost 1.6 kilometers (1 mile) deep and 29 kilometers (18 miles) wide in some places. A canyon that large takes millions of years to form.

Some canyons form because of the movement of ice and wind. However, the main way that canyons form is through the movement of rivers.

It took millions of years for the Colorado River to form the Grand Canyon.

River sediment was deposited to form this delta.

How does deposition cause deltas and sand dunes?

As water flows, it washes away sediment. But where does this sediment go? Remember that eroded sediments are dropped in new areas. The deposition of the sediment that flows along in rivers may cause deltas to form. A delta is a low, flat area of land. A delta is formed from sediment that is carried downstream by a river. The end of the river is usually where it meets ocean water. The river flows into the ocean, but the sediment is left behind. It collects at the end of the river as a delta.

A sand dune is another landform that is caused by deposition. A sand dune is a large deposit of sand that is moved by wind. In areas where there is a lot of sand, such as beaches and deserts, wind carries sand and deposits it.

Sand dunes are always changing. Wind sweeps and lifts sand up one side of the dune. Then gravity causes the sand to fall down the other side of the dune. Windstorms often occur on beaches and in deserts. These storms change the size and form of sand dunes often.

Wind works quickly to move sand, but it works slowly to move rock. It takes very long periods of time for wind to wear away rock, breaking off tiny particles.

Sand dunes in deserts are much larger than sand dunes on beaches.

How is sedimentary rock formed?

The processes of weathering, erosion, and deposition also help form layers of rock. These layers of rock can tell us about Earth's history.

You know that rock is weathered by water, wind, and ice. You know that sediment is carried away and deposited. But another process can then happen. Earth materials have not finished changing even after they have been deposited and have started to settle. A different and very slow process begins that forms layers of rock called sedimentary rock.

The layers of sediment in these rocks don't all look the same. They form stripes of different shades. Each of these rock layers tells about Earth's history.

Every layer of this rock was formed during a different time period.

Sedimentary rock forms when a layer of sediment is deposited somewhere. The weight squeezes the particles of sediment together. Then more sediment is deposited on top of the layer below. This puts extra weight on the lower layers. This pressure is so strong that water is pushed out of the sediment. Over time, minerals wear away and are deposited in the spaces between the sediments. This acts like a glue and binds the sediments together. Over millions of years, this sediment is put under so much pressure that it binds into rock.

Each layer of sedimentary rock is formed during a different period of Earth's history. The color of the sediment is different in each layer. This is because the minerals in the sediment are different at different time periods.

How are fossils formed?

Sedimentary rock layers can tell scientists about Earth's history. The lower layers of rock were formed millions of years earlier than the higher layers. Scientists can find traces of once-living organisms in the layers. A fossil is the remains or traces of a plant or an animal that lived long ago.

Fossils form in different ways. A mold is an impression of an organism. It is formed when sediment hardens around the organism's remains. The remains then decay or dissolve. An impression is the form that something makes when it presses into something. If a shell were pressed into sediment, the shape of the shell would show in the sediment. It would harden as if it were printed into the rock. The shell's shape and texture would be left in the rock.

Fossils are formed in layers of sedimentary rock.

A mold is an impression in the rock. A cast is a model that forms when sediment fills a mold and hardens.

A cast is a model of an organism. A cast is formed when sediment fills a mold and hardens. It takes a long time for a cast fossil to form. Sediment and minerals must build up inside a mold in order to form a cast.

Not all dead organisms become fossils. Many plants and animals simply decay over time. To become a fossil in sedimentary rock, the organism must die in or near water, where sediment is found. The sediment must quickly cover the organism. Most animal fossils are bones. That's because other parts of the animal are soft. They decay, leaving just the hard parts.

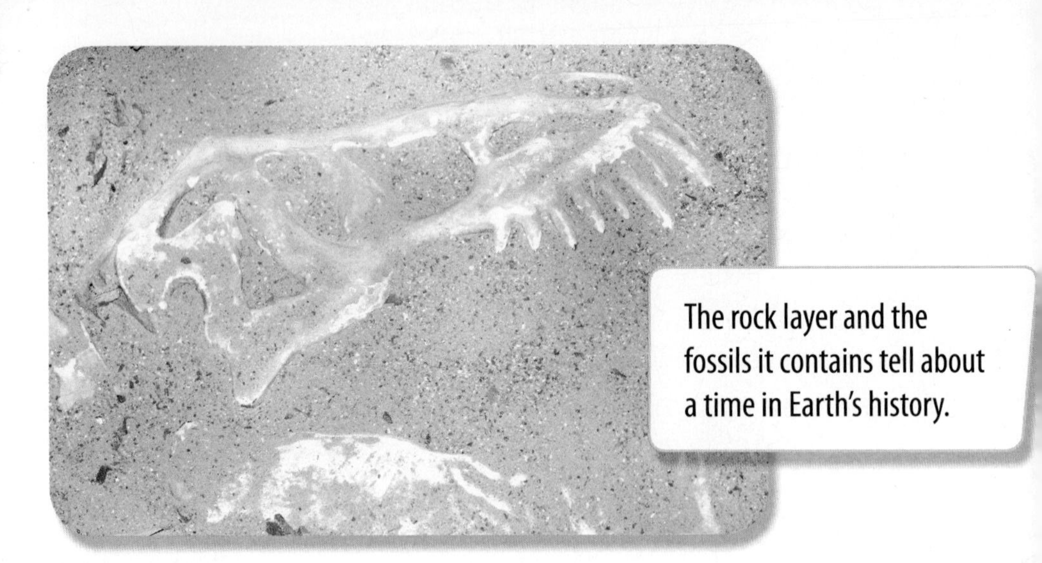

The rock layer and the fossils it contains tell about a time in Earth's history.

What can fossils tell us about organisms of the past?

Fossils give scientists important information about the past. The fossils in a rock layer can provide information about the living things during a part of Earth's history. The layer of rock is a record of that time on Earth. The layer is also a history of the plants and animals that lived at that time.

Earth's layers often shift to new positions. The layers can become tilted and lifted by earthquakes and other movements of Earth's plates. As a result, scientists have uncovered fossils from very deep layers of sedimentary rock.

Scientists first find out the time period that each layer of rock comes from. Then they can know the time period from which the fossils in that layer came.

Scientists can learn what organisms of the past looked like. They have pieced together whole dinosaurs based on what parts were found and where they were found.

Looking at fossils can help scientists understand important facts about time periods. For example, scientists know when trees that produce seeds in cones first appeared on Earth. If an animal fossil comes from this same time, the scientists have one clue about what the animal might have eaten. By putting clues together, scientists can try to figure out what the animals in a certain time period ate and how they behaved.

Index fossils can help scientists identify when a rock layer was formed.

Index fossils are fossils of organisms that lived during the same fairly short time period in many parts of the world. When they lived, there were many of these organisms. They were spread over wide areas. Trilobites are examples of these kinds of organisms. Scientists can use index fossils to figure out the age of a rock layer.

How do organisms of the past compare to organisms today?

Scientists can also use fossils to compare animals of today to animals of the past. Scientists can compare birds today to the fossils of dinosaurs that flew. This could give a hint about how animals have changed over millions of years.

When scientists find all or most fossil parts of an organism, they may be able to make a model. A model can show what the organism's skeleton looked like. They can then compare the body parts to those of similar animals today. Scientists can compare the size of an ancient fish's jaw to the jaw of a fish today. They can measure the length of an ancient mammal's limbs to see if they are longer or shorter than mammals' limbs today. All of these measurements give information about ways that organisms have changed over time.

Today's shrimp do not look very different from ancient shrimp.

By studying where each kind of fossil is found in rock layers, scientists can learn what kind of environment the plant or animal lived in. Then scientists can compare those environments to the places where similar organisms live today.

Scientists also use trace fossils to learn about animals that lived in the past. A trace fossil is not a body part. Instead, it is evidence of an organism's existence. It could be a footprint or a hole dug in the ground. Trace fossils are clues that can help scientists figure out how organisms behaved, how they moved, and how they lived with other organisms. Trace fossils can also reveal which of today's organisms the plants or animals were most like.

A trace fossil gives scientists clues about how animals behaved.

What can fossils tell us about Earth's history?

Fossils can help to tell Earth's long history. The layers of fossils that scientists uncover can show when big changes occurred on Earth.

The fossil record shows that many areas that are now dry land were once under water. Fossils of water plants and water animals can even be found on tops of mountains today. Fossils of trees are sometimes found where there are no trees today. These are all hints about Earth's past.

The fossils and sediment from each time period help us to learn more about Earth's timeline. Similar fossils from the same time period are often found in places that are very far apart. These discoveries help support scientists' hypothesis that the continents were connected millions of years ago.

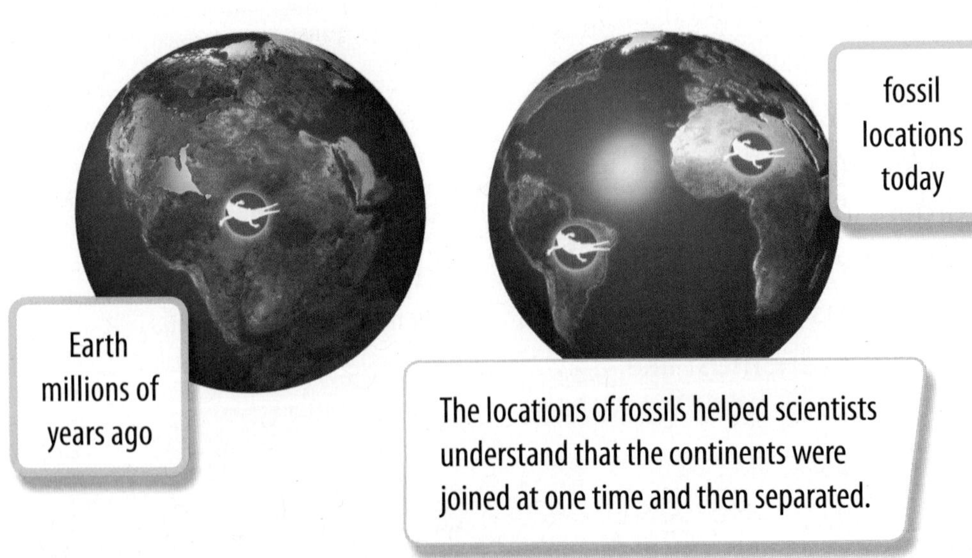

The locations of fossils helped scientists understand that the continents were joined at one time and then separated.

Fossil records also indicate when species have died off. A **mass extinction** is a period in which a large number of species disappear. By looking at fossils, scientists see that mass extinctions have taken place several times in Earth's past. Scientists can then hypothesize about the causes.

A large amount of volcanic ash may be found in the same rock layer that shows evidence of mass extinction. Volcanic eruptions could have changed the climate of the planet. They might have killed off many species because the organisms could not adjust to the change. An asteroid impact could also have changed the climate of Earth and caused a mass extinction. The clues that scientists gather from the fossil record help explain what might have caused the mass extinctions.

When large objects from space hit Earth, they give off a lot of dust. The dust can block sunlight for all living things.

What happens when organisms do not become fossils?

Most living things don't turn into fossils after they die. The remains of some organisms go through chemical changes that turn them into fossil fuels. A fossil fuel is an energy source, such as oil or natural gas, that is formed from the remains of once-living things.

For example, coal forms from dead plants. Sediment covers plants that have fallen to the bottom of a lake or pond. Pressure builds as more layers of sediment are added. Temperatures rise. The organisms' remains turn into a material called peat. The peat keeps getting pressed and heated. The water is squeezed out. Over millions of years, coal forms. When coal is removed from the ground, it can be burned for energy.

Plants die and settle under water. Then temperature and pressure cause peat to form. More pressure and heat cause coal to form.

Coal is being formed right now in peat bogs around the world. It will be a very long time before the peat becomes coal.

Tiny sea organisms settled to the ocean floor millions of years ago. Pressure and layers of sediment turned the organisms into oil and natural gas. Pumps remove oil and natural gas from the ground so that we can burn them as fuel.

Pumps bring oil and natural gas to the surface to be burned.

Earth's surface is always changing. Because of the processes of weathering, erosion, and deposition, Earth's surface will always be changing.

Responding

Make Fossil Models

Work with a partner to make models of fossils. One of you should make a cast. The other should make a mold. Use clay and everyday objects to form your fossils. Display your work for the class. Explain the difference between a cast and a mold.

Draw a Poster

How do the processes of weathering and erosion take place? What kinds of landforms are a result of these changes to Earth's surface? Work with a partner to make a poster that explains how one change to Earth's surface occurs. Draw a diagram. Include labels that explain the steps of the process. Display your work.

Glossary

cast [KAST] A model of an organism, formed when sediment fills a mold and hardens. *The scientist found a cast of an ancient insect.*

deposition [dep•uh•ZISH•uhn] The dropping or settling of eroded materials. *The rushing river causes deposition to occur downstream.*

erosion [i•ROH•zhuhn] The process of moving sediment from one place to another. *The storm caused a lot of erosion to occur on the beach.*

fossil [FAHS•uhl] The remains or traces of a plant or an animal that lived long ago. *A fossil can be found in layers of rock.*

fossil fuel [FAHS•uhl FYOO•uhl] Fuel, such as coal, oil, and natural gas, formed from the remains of once-living things. *Coal, oil, and natural gas are fossil fuels.*

index fossil [IN•deks FAHS•uhl] A fossil of a type of organism that lived in many places during a relatively short time span. *Trilobites and ferns are examples of index fossils.*

mass extinction [MAS ek•STINGK•shuhn] A period in which a large number of species become extinct. *One of the most famous mass extinctions is the disappearance of dinosaurs.*

mold [MOHLD] An impression of an organism, formed when sediment hardens around the organism. *The scientist discovered a mold of a tree leaf in a rock layer.*

sedimentary rock [SED•uh•MEN•tuh•ree RAHK] A type of rock that forms when layers of sediment are pressed together. *Fossils of living things from long ago are found in sedimentary rock.*

weathering [WETH•er•ing] The breaking down of rocks on Earth's surface into smaller pieces. *Wind, ice, and water can cause weathering.*